FUZZY BROWN

Finds A Home

TO KENDALL....
WISHING YOU WARM
FUZZY BROWN DAYS.
SANDY 2005

Written & Illustrated by Sandy Rudnick

SANDY RUDNICK

Fuzzy Brown Productions
P.O. Box 120
Bakersfield, CA 93302

Printed in the USA
ISBN 1-933192-00-3
Library of Congress Catalog number 2004115046

This book is for Grandma Kearney and all the "Fuzzy Browns" of the world.

The Story of Fuzzy Brown

Grandma Kearney with Fuzzy Brown and friends.

This is a story based on the life of a little shaggy dog. He was an abandoned Lhasa Apso and was found at a middle school many years ago in 1985. I was at the school taking my son his lunch and the nice SPCA man had this cute little dog in his truck, and he asked me if I wanted him. "Sure" I said, but in my mind I thought, "I'll find him a good home," and I did. I kept him myself!

We named him Fuzzy Brown and he lived with us and was shared with my family. He then lived with my mother, who was called Grandma Kearney, in Bakersfield California and spent his summers with Grandma on Orcas Island in Washington State. Later, when Grandma moved into a retirement home, Fuzzy Brown went as well. He was a special character to everyone and he gave and received a great deal of love and affection. Fuzzy moved back in with me after my mother passed away in 2001. Fuzzy Brown was known and loved by all.

The little brown dog heard children playing.

They were happy sounds.

He walked closer to
the schoolyard
and saw the
children playing.

"I want to be with children because
they are having fun," he said.

and onto the schoolyard.

The children ran over
and looked at him.

"He is a cute little brown dog!"
they exclaimed. "Where did he
come from? Who does he
belong to and where does he live?"

The children
wanted to know.

The bell rang calling the children inside the classroom.

The little brown dog was all alone again.

"I will wait until the children return," said the lonely little brown dog. I am tired and hungry," he barked.

Soon the school janitor came along pushing a broom.

"Well, well," he said.
"You're a cute little dog.
Where is your collar?
Where are your tags?

They would tell me your
name and where you live."

"You must be hungry," said the janitor.
"Would you like to share my sandwich?"

The little brown dog gobbled the sandwich and then followed the janitor down the hallway. "We must go to the principal's office," said the janitor. "Mrs. Goodness will know what to do."

"I know! Let's call the SPCA," suggested Mrs. Goodness. "They love dogs and cats and they will help find this cute little brown dog a good home."

"You are a cute little brown dog," agreed the kind SPCA man. "Come with me. We will give you a warm bath and good food."

The children waved good-bye as
the little brown dog left the
schoolyard with the
nice SPCA man.

"Good-bye little
brown dog, Good-bye,"
the children called.
"We will miss you!"

"I know just the perfect home for you!"

exclaimed the helpful SPCA man.

"I will call Mrs. Duckwater. She is looking for a small dog and would give you a nice home."

When Mrs. Duckwater saw him she agreed. "Well, you are a cute little fuzzy brown dog. I think I will take you home with me!"

"What should I name him?" thought Mrs. Duckwater.

"I know what I will name him.

Fuzzy Brown

That's it,

Fuzzy Brown!"

Fuzzy Brown and
Mrs. Duckwater
said good-bye to the
nice SPCA man.

Fuzzy Brown hopped
into Mrs. Duckwater's
car and they drove
to a pretty house
on a hill. This was
Fuzzy Brown's new home.

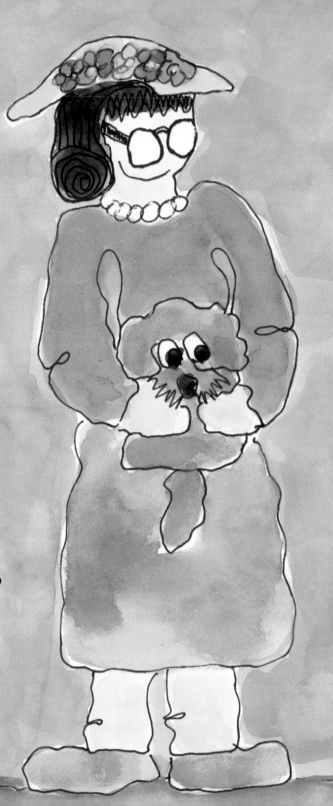

About Fuzzy's Author

Sandy Rudnick paints in acrylics and watercolors. She lives with her husband, Richard, in Bakersfield, California where they raise cattle and horses in the southern Sierra Nevada Mountains. Her children, Chad, Jane, and Jack were raised with numerous pets including many dogs and cats. Sandy's love of animals is reflected in her art!

Art Direction and layout by
Greg Bell, Altitude Design.

A portion of the proceeds from this book are donated to the SPCA to help all the Fuzzy Browns of the world.

SPCA Society for the Prevention of Cruelty to Animals